This edition published by Parragon in 2012
Parragon
Queen Street House
4 Queen Street
Bath BA1 1HE, UK
www.parragon.com

Edited by Samantha Crockford
Designed by Pete Hampshire
Production by Emma Fulleylove

ISBN 978-1-4454-7394-9

Printed in China

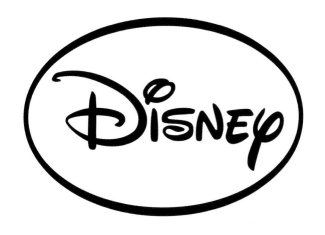

Disney

STORYBOOK COLLECTION

PaRragon

Bath • New York • Singapore • Hong Kong • Cologne • Delhi
Melbourne • Amsterdam • Johannesburg • Auckland • Shenzhen

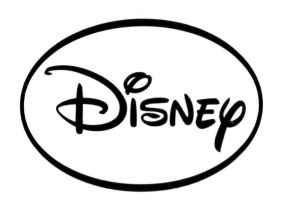

This book belongs to

....

CONTENTS

Mickey Mouse Clubhouse
A Hot Dog Day   11

Agent OSO
Bananas Are Forever   67

Mickey Mouse Clubhouse
Farmer Donald's Pumpkin Patch   99

Jungle Junction
The Circus Comes to Town   125

A HOT DOG DAY

Things for Picnic:
Tablecloth
Napkins

Plates
Fruit Salad
Lemonade
Corn on the Cob
Hot Dogs
Buns
Ketchup
Mustard

By Sheila Sweeny Higginson
Illustrated by the Disney Storybook Artists

Minnie woke up early. She opened the window to let in the cool morning air. Outside, the birds were chirping. The sun peeked through the trees on the horizon.

"What a lovely day!" Minnie said. "It's the perfect day for a picnic. The first thing I need to do is make invitations."

Minnie looked over the invitations she had made. "My friends will be so happy to receive these pretty cards," she said. Then she sat down and wrote a list of all the things she would need for the picnic – a tablecloth, plates, napkins and food, of course! When she was finished, she headed out of the door.

But before she had gone very far, she turned around.

"Silly me," she said. "I forgot to bring something to hold all my picnic goodies. And I really should bring along my new tablecloth, and napkins and some plates. Then I won't have to come back for them later."

Minnie looked around the Clubhouse for something that was big enough for all the picnic supplies. She soon found her basket on a high shelf.

"But how will I reach it?" Minnie asked. "Should I use a fishhook and try to reel it in? Or could I lasso it with that rope?" she wondered aloud, looking at the rope that was hanging on the wall.

"Mmm," she finally said, "maybe using this stepladder would be the best choice."

Minnie carefully climbed the ladder. She took the basket from the shelf and climbed back down. Then she placed the chequered tablecloth, napkins and plates inside the basket.

Minnie headed outdoors. When she reached the Clubhouse garden, she exclaimed, "These flowers are so pretty! I'll make a bouquet."

She thought the flowers would make a lovely centrepiece for the picnic table. Before delivering her invitations or shopping for the picnic food, she decided to go back to the Clubhouse and put the flowers in a vase filled with water.

So, off she went, back to the Clubhouse, leaving her picnic basket on the lawn.

A moment later, Daisy strolled by. There on the lawn, she saw Minnie's picnic basket.

"What's this?" she wondered aloud. "Minnie is planning a picnic? I love picnics!"

Daisy read Minnie's shopping list and decided to make a fruit salad to share with all the guests. She picked up the basket and headed towards the blueberry bushes at the end of the road.

19

Before long, Daisy had picked many, many blueberries. She filled her handbag with them. She tasted a few, just to make sure they were sweet enough for her friends.

"Oh, my," she said to herself when she could hold no more berries. "I need to get a bowl – one that's big enough to hold all the fruit for the salad."

So off she went, leaving the basket under a bush.

21

Minnie returned to the garden. She saw that her picnic basket was missing!

"My picnic basket!" she cried. "Where could it be?"

Minnie looked behind the daffodils. She looked under the tulips. She retraced her steps back to the Clubhouse. But she could not find it.

"Oh, no!" Minnie said, sighing. "My picnic is over, and it never even started!" Sadly, she plopped into a chair.

Even the flowers looked glum.

Back in the kitchen, Daisy found a small bowl, but the bowl was not large enough to hold the berries. So she poured them into a medium-size bowl. That, too, soon overflowed. Finally, Daisy put all the blueberries into a large bowl.

"Perfect!" she said. "There's even room left over for me to add some watermelon."

Daisy headed out the door, thinking about the delicious fruit salad she would soon make for her friends.

Daisy went to the watermelon patch behind the Clubhouse. There were six juicy watermelons growing on the vine. She looked at them all and decided not to take the biggest one.

"That one would be too heavy for me to lift," she said to herself.

She decided not to take the smallest one. "That one would not have enough juicy fruit inside."

She didn't pick any of the yellow ones, either, because yellow melons need more time to grow.

She wondered aloud, "Which one is just right?"

Daisy did not choose the biggest or the smallest or any of the yellow melons. That left just one – the medium-sized green melon. Daisy cut it open and was very happy to see juicy red fruit inside.

"This melon smells so sweet!" she declared as she carefully cut the fruit into cubes.

As Daisy mixed her salad, Donald was taking a walk down the road near the blueberry bush. He spotted a basket and looked inside.

"Well, finally!" Donald exclaimed. "Someone is planning a picnic! And best of all, there will be lemonade at the picnic. I love lemonade." Donald decided that he would make the lemonade himself.

Taking the basket with him, Donald headed off into town to buy the ingredients for his lemonade.

Things for Picnic:
Tablecloth
Napkins
Plates
Fruit Salad
Lemonade
Corn on the Cob
of Dogs
uns
chup

Daisy finished mixing the blueberries and the watermelon in the bowl.

"All that this salad needs to be perfect," she announced, "is something yellow." She remembered that there was a pineapple in the kitchen.

Before getting the pineapple, Daisy looked around for Minnie's basket.

"Oh, no! Where could it be?" she cried. She tried to remember where she had seen it last.

"The blueberry bush!" she shouted as she ran down the road.

Daisy looked under the blueberry bush. She looked next to the blueberry bush. She even looked behind the blueberry bush. But she could not find Minnie's basket.

"I guess I should just make a fruit salad for everyone," Daisy said to herself.

Donald couldn't wait to make his special lemonade. He arrived at the grocery shop carrying the basket and the list.

"Well, let me see," he said. "I'll buy some sugar and a jar of red cherries. And I'll need six lemons – and my secret ingredient: one lime."

Donald looked at the lemons. He thought they all looked delicious. But one seemed especially plump and juicy. Donald reached for the biggest lemon.

"Not that one!" the shopkeeper shouted to Donald. "Don't take one from the bottom because –"

But it was too late. The lemons fell down on Donald and tumbled onto the floor. Donald quickly ran out of the door after buying his lemons, and left Minnie's basket behind.

Donald headed back to the Clubhouse.

"My goodness!" he quacked, looking in the windows. "Minnie and Daisy
sure do look grumpy. Well, they'll feel better when I serve them my super-duper,
secret-recipe lemonade."

Donald cut each lemon – and one lime – in half. He squeezed each half in the juicer. Next, he slid a straw through each cherry and mixed some cherry juice in with the lemon and lime juice. Then he measured out the right amount of sugar, poured water into the pitcher, added the juice and some ice, and stirred.

"This is guaranteed to perk up my grumpy friends!"

On this sunny morning, Goofy was in town, taking his kitten, Mr Pettibone, for a walk. When Mr Pettibone spotted a lemon rolling down the pavement, he pounced on it.

Goofy looked inside the shop and saw the shopkeeper picking up all the rolling lemons. He began to help. Just as he was about to pick up the last lemon, something caught his eye.

It was Minnie's basket with a letter addressed to him.

"Oh, boy!" Goofy said when he read the invitation. "There's nothing I like more than a picnic!"

He looked at the shopping list. "Seems to me that someone needs to make some corn on the cob. There's nothing I like more than corn on the cob – except picnics!" he said. So, off he went towards the cornfield, taking the basket with him.

Goofy

Goofy walked quickly down the road towards the cornfield. The corn had grown high under the warm sun. It was even taller than he was! As he approached the rows of stalks, Goofy could almost taste the corn.

"Look at those big ears!" he exclaimed, wetting his lips.

Things for Picnic:
~~Tablecloth~~
~~Napkins~~
~~Plates~~
~~Fruit Salad~~
~~Lemonade~~
~~Corn on the Cob~~
Hot Dogs

"How many cobs do we need?" Goofy wondered aloud. "Well, Pluto doesn't eat corn, so I don't need to count him. Minnie will want one. Daisy will want one. That's two, so far. Donald will probably have two. So, two plus two equals four. Mickey will want one. That's five. And I'll have five. So all together, I need to pick ten ears of corn."

Goofy was so excited about getting back to the Clubhouse to cook the corn, that he left the basket behind! He was so happy that he sang a corny little song as he walked:

Corn, corn, wonderful corn.
I could eat it night and morn!
Cornflakes, corn bread, corn dogs, too.
Corn on the cob for me and you!

Goofy looked in the kitchen for the largest pot he could find. He filled it with water and waited until the water boiled.

Meanwhile, Donald had gone into the garden to pick a few mint leaves to add to the lemonade. He thought it would be a good idea to put the pitcher into Minnie's basket. He looked around.

"Uh, oh," he said. "Where's the basket? Could I have left it at the shop?"

Donald ran back to town. At the shop, he looked under the counter. He looked behind the new stack of lemons. "This is terrible!" he whispered to himself when he realized that the picnic basket was gone. Then he tiptoed outside and headed back to the Clubhouse.

Meanwhile, Mickey and Pluto were out for a drive. There was only one thing Pluto liked more than riding in Mickey's car, and that was running through the cornfield. So Mickey stopped the car to give Pluto a chance to run around.

"What's this?" Mickey said when he saw the basket. He recognized it right away.

"This is Minnie's basket," he said, picking it up. Then he saw the invitations inside. "Hey, Pluto!" he called. "Minnie is having a picnic, and we're invited! Let's get these last things on her list before heading back to the Clubhouse."

Back at the Clubhouse kitchen, Goofy placed the corn in hot water, along with a pinch of sugar and a dash of salt.

"I think I'll put this plate of corn into Minnie's basket now," Goofy said. That's when he realized that he'd left the basket back at the cornfield.

Goofy ran out of the door, straight towards the cornfield. He looked high. He looked low. Then he looked very, very sad.

"Gawrsh!" he said, "I feel just awful about losing Minnie's basket." Slowly, he walked back towards the Clubhouse with his long ears hanging down.

47

At the shop, Mickey piled the hot dogs, buns, ketchup and mustard onto the counter.

"Well, that's about it, Pluto," he said. Then he glanced at the clock.

"Golly! It's almost noon. We'd better hurry back to the Clubhouse for Minnie's picnic."

Out of the door they went.

It was almost lunchtime, but Minnie wasn't hungry.

"The next time I plan a picnic," she said to herself, "I'll make sure that I don't lose the invitations and the picnic basket!" She decided to take a walk. "Maybe I can pretend I'm having a picnic with my friends," she said. She took along her flowers.

At almost the same moment, Daisy decided to take her bowl
of fruit salad to the picnic table.

"Maybe some of my friends will be at the playground
and would like to share this salad," she sighed.

Donald remembered that the picnic was planned for noon
at the playground, so he grabbed his pitcher and headed out.
"All you really need for a picnic is my special lemonade,"
Donald said to himself.

Goofy, too, decided to bring his plate of corn to the playground.

"Golly, I sure hope the picnic is still on," he said as he walked towards the picnic area. Then he smiled and said, "Otherwise, I guess I'll have to eat all this corn myself."

"Looks like we're just in time, old buddy," Mickey said to Pluto as they neared the playground.

"I hope we're not too late, Minnie," Mickey said as he walked towards his friends.
Minnie was speechless while her friends set the table.

Finally, she said, "I lost my basket and all the invitations in the garden this morning.
So I thought my picnic was ruined."

"I'm sorry," Daisy said.
"I found your basket in the
garden and decided to
make a fruit salad."

"But then I lost it by
the blueberry bush."

"Well, actually, I found your basket by the blueberry bush," Donald said. "And I decided to make lemonade. But then I lost the basket at the grocery shop."

"I found it at the grocery shop,"
Goofy said. "And I decided to make
corn on the cob. But then I left your
basket in the cornfield."

"Pluto and I found your basket in the cornfield," Mickey said, "and we decided to get the hot dogs, buns and fixings."

Then he turned to Minnie and said, "I hope you're not angry with us, Minnie."

62

"How could I be angry?" Minnie said as she looked at all of her friends and the tasty foods they had made for her picnic. "You're the best friends in the whole world."

Everyone enjoyed Daisy's fruit salad, Donald's lemonade, Goofy's corn on the cob and the wonderful hot dogs and buns that Mickey prepared.

"This is the best picnic ever!" Minnie declared.

"Hot dog!" Mickey agreed.

The End

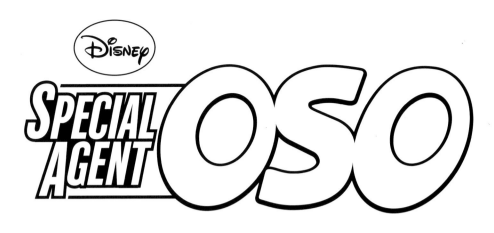

BANANAS ARE FOREVER

Written by Bill Scollon
Illustrated by Alan Batson

Special Agent Oso stands at the edge of a cliff, high up in the mountains.

"It looks like the only way to get to the other side is by walking across this narrow beam," he says.

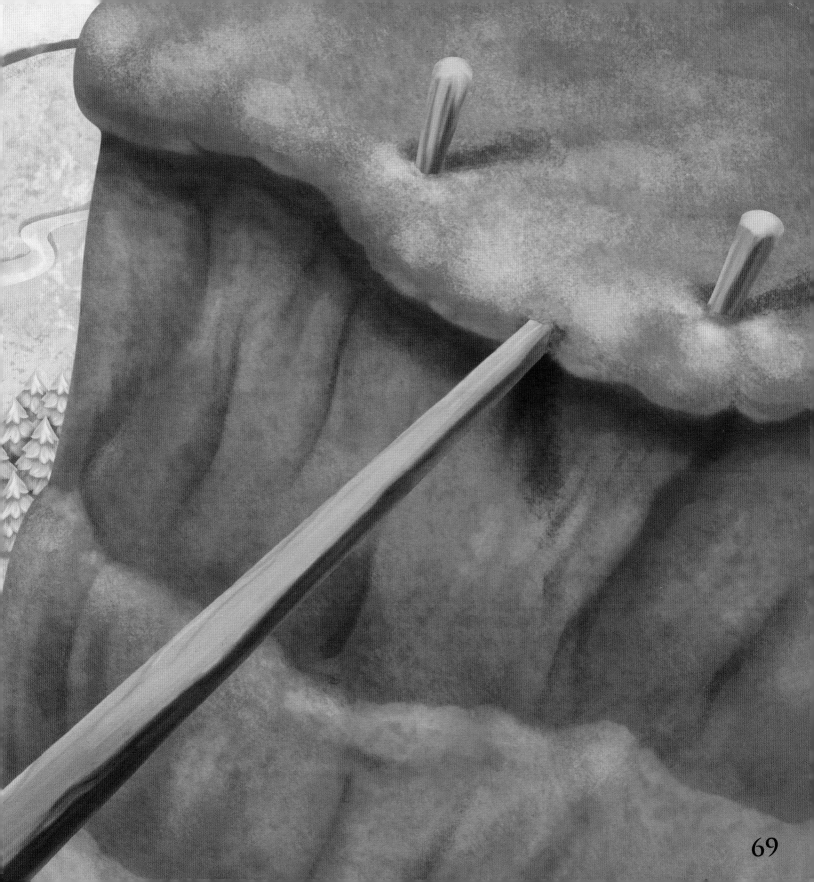

"Today's training exercise is balance-beam crossing. Whirly Bird will hold your safety line," says Special Agent Dotty.

"This exercise will test your balance," says Dotty.

"Watch where you put your feet."

"If I go one step at a time," Oso whispers, "I'm sure I can do it!"

Meanwhile, Keira is excited that her friends Maya and Toni are coming over.

"Let's make a snack for them!" Keira says.

"We'll make a yummy, healthy snack, right after I give the baby a bath," says Keira's mum.

"But Mama," says Keira, "they'll be here soon!"

"Start without me," says Keira's mum.

"But I don't know how to make a healthy snack," Keira says.

Shutter Bug sees that Keira needs help!

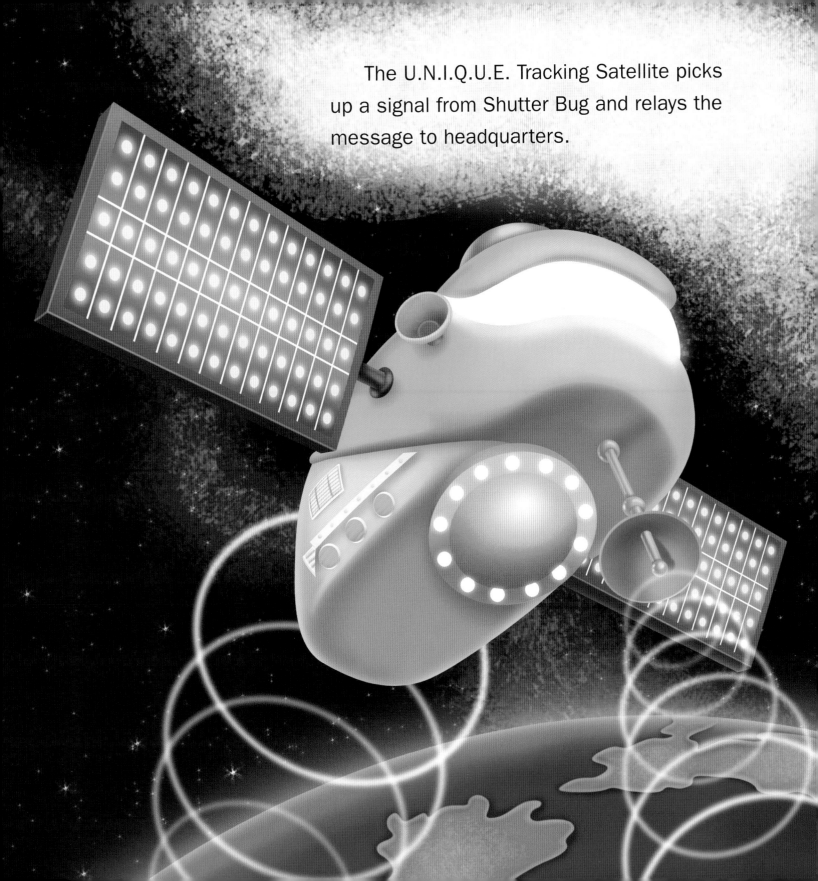

The U.N.I.Q.U.E. Tracking Satellite picks up a signal from Shutter Bug and relays the message to headquarters.

Special Agent Oso is halfway across the beam.

"I wish I could remember what Dotty told me to watch," says Oso.

All of a sudden, Oso's watch pops open and he loses his balance! It's his boss, Mister Dos, calling.

"Hurry, Oso!" says Mister Dos. "Keira must prepare a healthy snack before her friends arrive. She needs your help."

"Whirly Bird will fly me to Keira's house," says Oso.
"The checklist will have three special steps to help Keira
make a healthy snack," says Paw Pilot.

"I see her house," says Oso.
"It's over there – near downtown."
"Did you say 'down-down'?"
asks Whirly Bird.

"Down, down you go!" Whirly Bird says.

"That's not what I said!" yells Oso. Whirly Bird drops
Oso out of the cockpit. Oso floats towards Keira's house.

"I'm here to help you make a healthy snack," says Oso. "Paw Pilot, what's the first step on the checklist?"

"Step one," says Paw Pilot, "is to look at the foods you have!"

"Let's look in the pantry," says Keira.

Agent Oso springs into action.

"Stand back, Keira!" Oso shouts. "We have no idea who or what is behind that door!"

"Sure we do," says Keira. "It's just food."

"Oh! I see lots of healthy choices," says Oso.

"Most of the food in the pantry needs to be cooked," Keira points out. "And I don't use the stove."

"Right," Oso says. "Your healthy snack should be a safe snack. No cooking and no sharp knives. This assignment is making me hungry."

"Here are more healthy foods to choose from!" exclaims Oso, looking in the refrigerator. "How about melon-and-cheese kebab or apple slices with yoghurt dip."

"Step one is complete," says Paw Pilot. "Now for step two. Decide on one thing to make."

"We can make frozen cinnamon bananas on a stick!" shouts Keira. "I had them at a friend's birthday party, and they're yummy!"

"Great job," says Paw Pilot. "You're ready for step three – prepare your healthy snack."

Keira and Oso begin making frozen cinnamon bananas.

Whoops! Oso drops a banana peel and steps right on it.
"Watch where you put your feet, Oso!" says Keira.

"Watch where I put my feet?" says Agent Oso.
"That's what Dotty told me to do!"

Agent Oso cuts the bananas into two pieces.

Keira puts a lollipop stick in each piece and sprinkles them with cinnamon.

"These will make terrific healthy snacks," says Oso.

"Hurry, Oso!" urges Paw Pilot. "You don't have much time!"

93

"They have to freeze for one hour,"
Keira says. "That's when my friends will be here."
"Step three completed," says Paw Pilot.

Keira tells her mum all about the healthy snack.

"Thank you, Agent Oso!" says Keira.

"Just doing my job!" he says.

"Keira reminded me of what Dotty said," says Agent Oso. "'Watch where I put my feet.' That helps a lot!"

"Great job, Oso!" says Dotty. "You've completed your training exercise."

"Well done!" says Mister Dos.

"That assignment had a certain appeal!" says Agent Oso.

The End

FARMER DONALD'S PUMPKIN PATCH

By Susan Ring
Illustrated by Loter, Inc.

"Look at this!" said Daisy as she came into the Clubhouse one day.
"This pumpkin won the grand prize at the County Fair!"
"Hot dog!" said Mickey. "That is one big pumpkin!"

Donald took a look at the picture.

"Aw, phooey!" he said. "I could grow a garden filled with the biggest pumpkins you've ever seen!" Donald declared. "I'm sure it's easy to do."

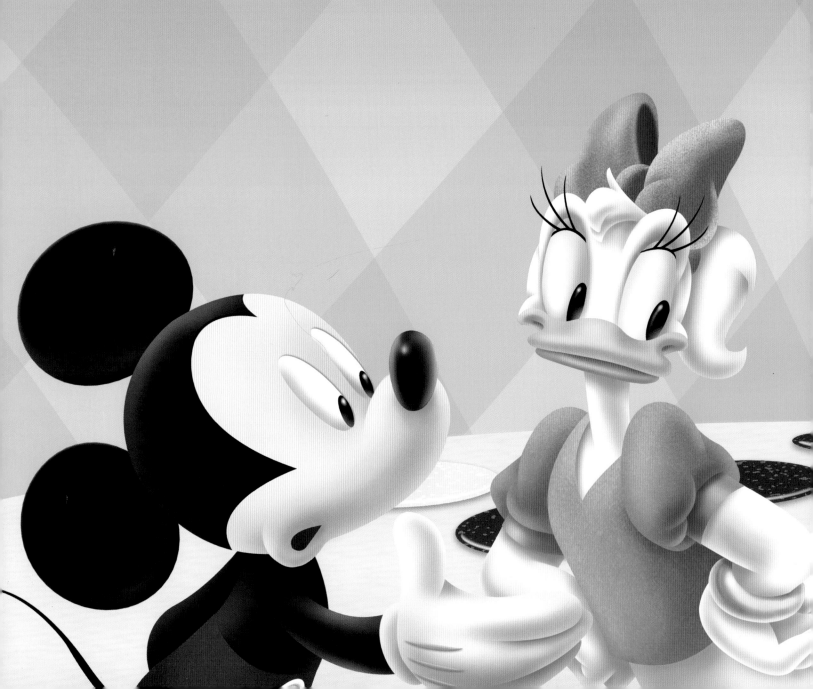

103

The next day, Donald got pumpkin seeds and threw them on the soil.

"I think it takes more than that to grow a garden," said Minnie.

Mickey nodded. "First you need to make holes in the soil, put a seed in each hole and then cover them up."

"That's a lot of work," said Donald.

"Maybe Toodles can help," said Mickey. "Oh, Toodles!"

Toodles showed them a pogo stick, a mirror and an elephant.

"Hmm," Donald said. "Which Mouseketool can help us make holes for the seeds?"

"I think it's this one," said Minnie, as she pointed to the pogo stick.

Minnie was right! The pogo stick made holes that were just the right size. Then Donald dropped a seed into each hole and covered them all with soil.

"See, I told you this would be easy," said Donald as he sat back down. "Now all we have to do is watch the seeds grow."

Donald, thinking his work was done, closed his eyes to rest.

"I think it takes more than that to grow a garden," said Daisy.

"A garden needs water," Mickey said. "Water helps seeds grow."

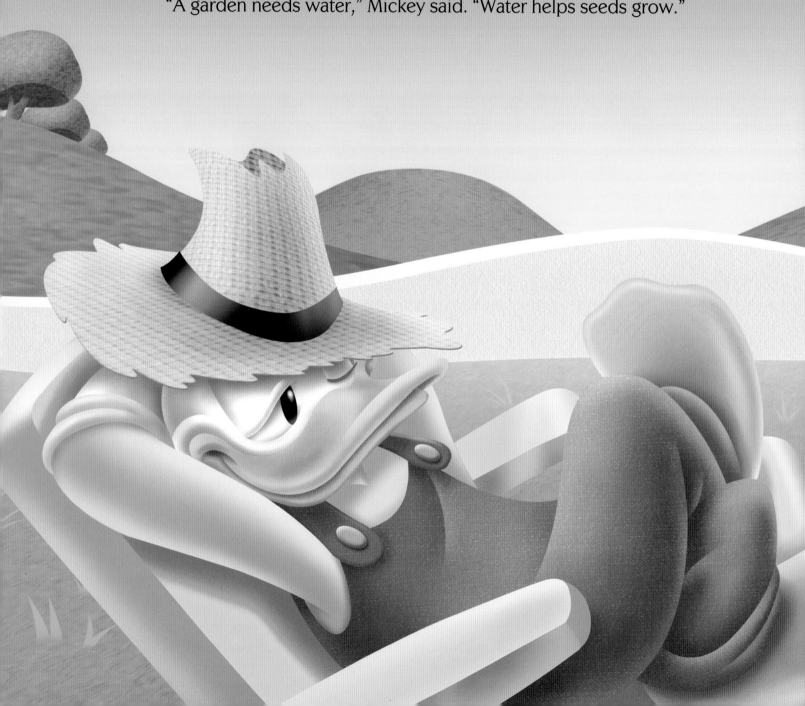

"Mickey's right," said Minnie.

"But how am I going to water this big garden?" asked Donald. "That's a lot of work."

"It's time to call Toodles again," said Mickey. "Oh, Toodles!"

"Let's pick the elephant," said Daisy, looking at the remaining tools.
Daisy was right! First the elephant took a big drink from the pond.
Then, using her trunk, she sprinkled water over the entire garden.

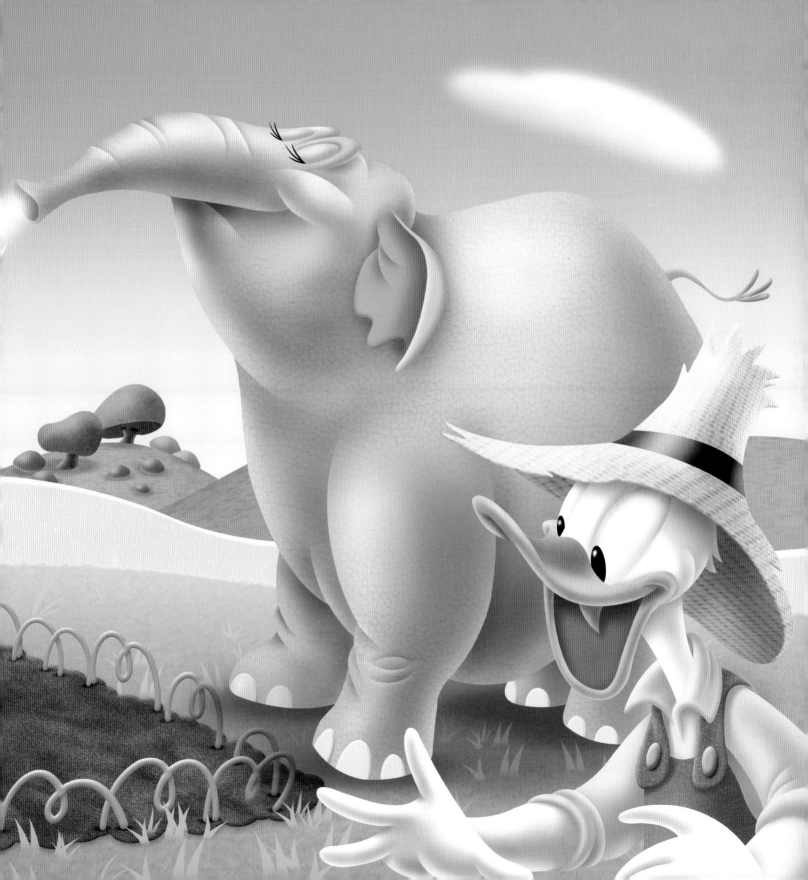

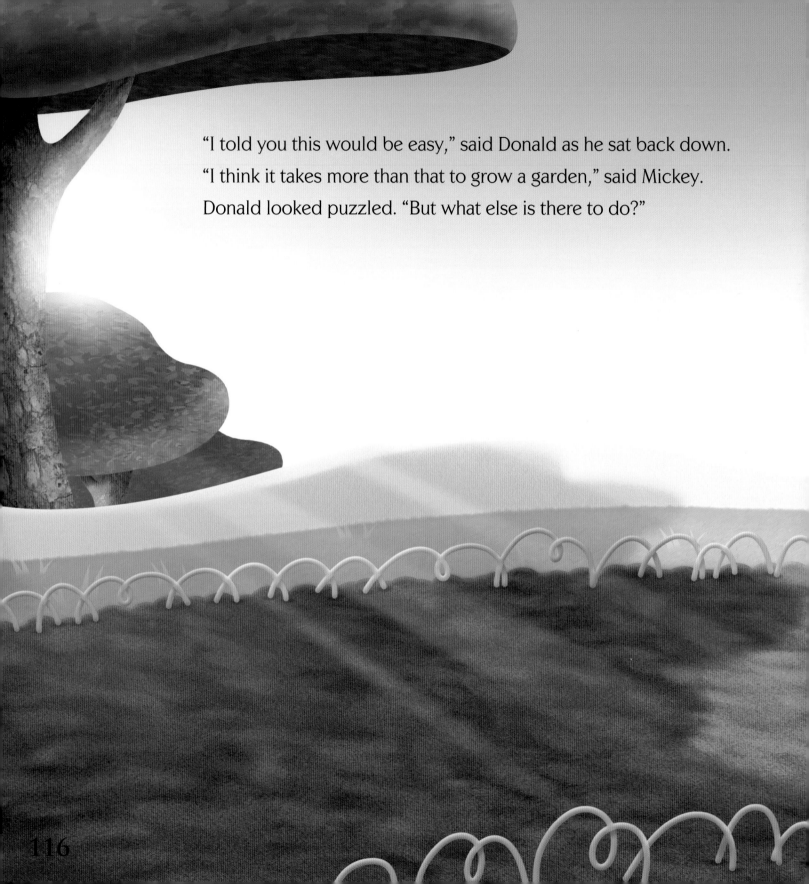

"I told you this would be easy," said Donald as he sat back down.

"I think it takes more than that to grow a garden," said Mickey.

Donald looked puzzled. "But what else is there to do?"

"Plants need sun," said Minnie. "But your garden is in the shade."

"But we can't move the sun!" exclaimed Donald.

"Maybe we can," said Mickey. "Oh, Toodles!"

Toodles had just one tool left – a mirror.

"A mirror?" asked Donald. "How can that help my garden grow?"

Mickey and Minnie placed the mirror so that it reflected the sunlight onto the garden.

"Oh, boy!" shouted Donald. "Now we'll just watch the seeds grow."

Daisy giggled. "Now we have to make sure the garden keeps getting plenty of water and sunlight and care, Farmer Donald!"

Donald discovered that growing a garden wasn't as easy as he expected. But over the next few months, he worked hard. When it was time for the pumpkin contest, Donald picked the biggest, most beautiful pumpkin from his garden, and then the whole gang headed to the fair.

Judge Goofy walked around and looked at all the pumpkins. Finally he said, "The prize for the biggest pumpkin goes to Farmer Donald!"

"Next year, I think I'll enter the apple-pie contest," said Daisy.

"Good idea!" Donald declared. "I'll plant a great big apple orchard so you'll have all the apples you need. I'm sure it's easy to do."

The End

123

THE CIRCUS
COMES TO TOWN

Written by Melinda LaRose
Illustrated by Alan Batson

Zip! Zoom!

Ellyvan and Zooter race through Jungle Junction.

Suddenly, Ellyvan stops. He sees a brand-new sign! What does it mean?

"The circus is coming to town!" says Zooter.

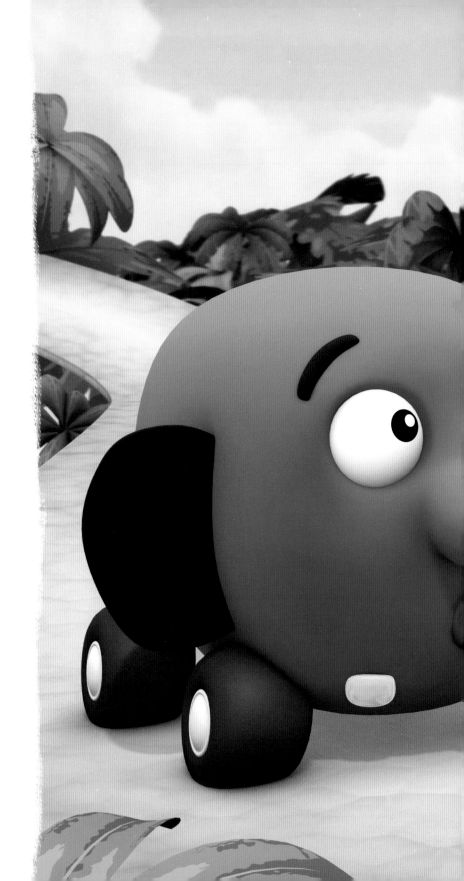

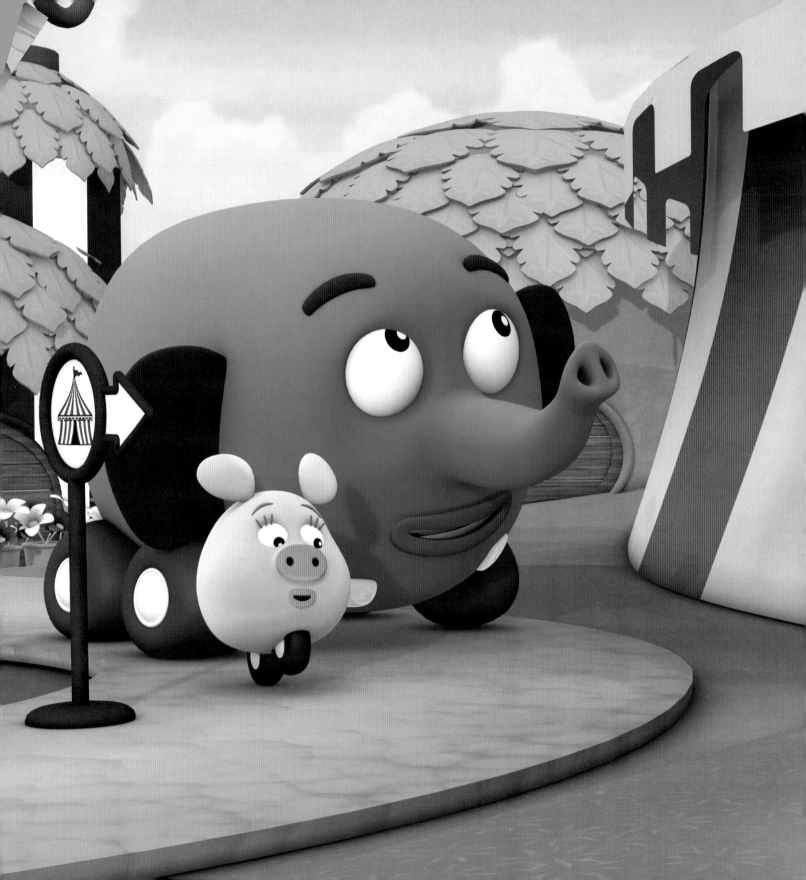

The sign leads to Miss Jolly's school.

"We can't wait to see your circus!" says Zooter.

"How would you like to be *in* my circus?" asks Miss Jolly.

"Wowie-zowie! I would love to!" says Zooter.

"Me, too! Me, too!" says Ellyvan.

What will Ellyvan and Zooter do in the circus?

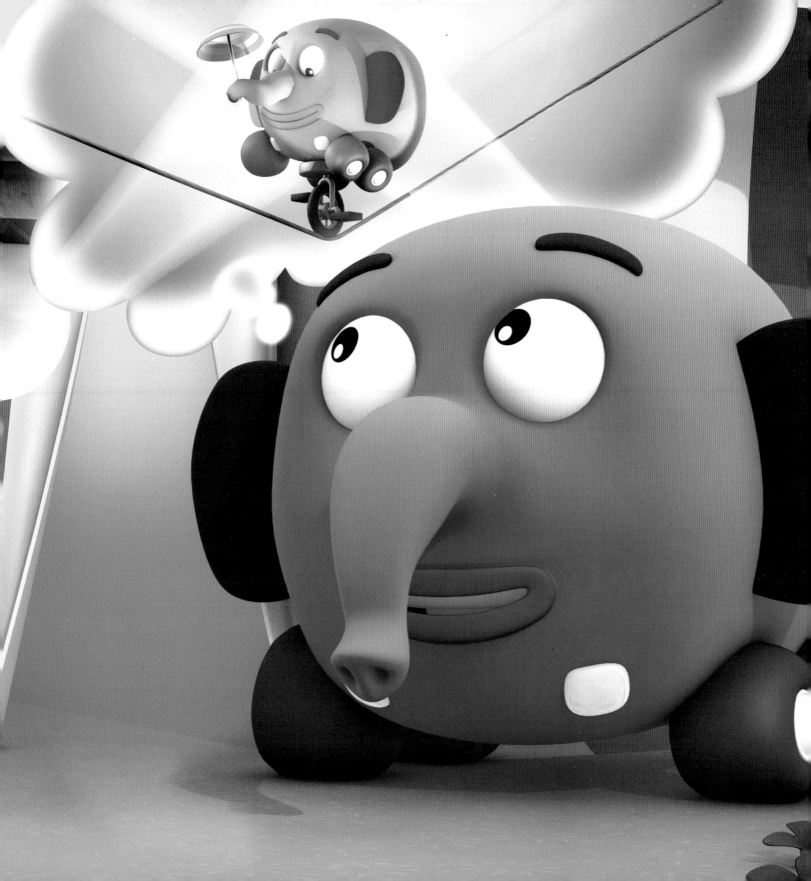

Taxicrab is the circus juggler.
"My juggling is as smooth as my smoothies!" says Taxicrab.
The Beetle Bugs are acrobats.
"Ta-da!" cry the Beetle Bugs.

"My two wheels are perfect for the high wire," says Zooter.
But what will Ellyvan do?

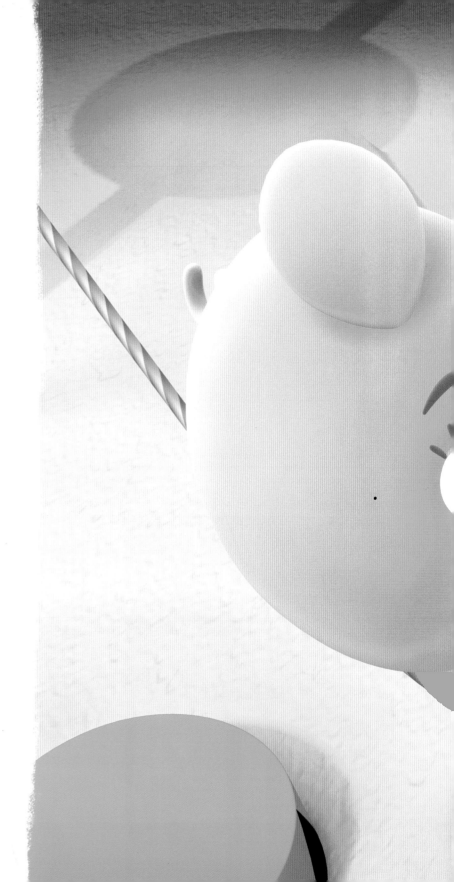

"How about the trapeze?" asks Bungo.
"You can soar through the air with the greatest of ease!"

Ellyvan closes his eyes and jumps off the platform!

THUD!

"Am I doing it?" asks Ellyvan.
"Not quite," says Bungo.

"How about the seesaw?" asks
Zooter. "You can tumble
and twirl!"

The Beetle Bugs jump on the seesaw.
Uh-oh! Ellyvan doesn't budge.

"Am I doing it?" asks Ellyvan.
"Not quite," says Zooter.

143

"Sorry, Miss Jolly. I guess I'm too big
for the circus," Ellyvan says sadly.

Just then, Taxicrab
trips and bumps
into the tent pole!
Whoa! The tent
is falling!

Ellyvan holds up the tent with his trunk!

"You saved the day," says Miss Jolly.

"And you found a circus act!" says Zooter.

"I did?" asks Ellyvan.

148

Miss Jolly starts the circus. "Presenting... the Jungle Junction Circus!"

Zip, zip! The Amazing Zooter rides the tightrope on one wheel!

Hup-hup! Taxicrab the Great can juggle anything! Even Toadhog!

151

Whoosh! Bungo the Magnificent flies over the crowd!

Boing-boing! **The Bouncing Beetle Bugs build a pyramid!**

"And now," announces Miss Jolly, "the strongest strongman in Jungle Junction – Ellyvan!"

"Am I doing it?" Ellyvan asks.
"You sure are!" says Zooter.

Bravo! The circus stars take their bows!
The Jungle Junction Circus is a big hit!

The End